THE CUTEST MULE

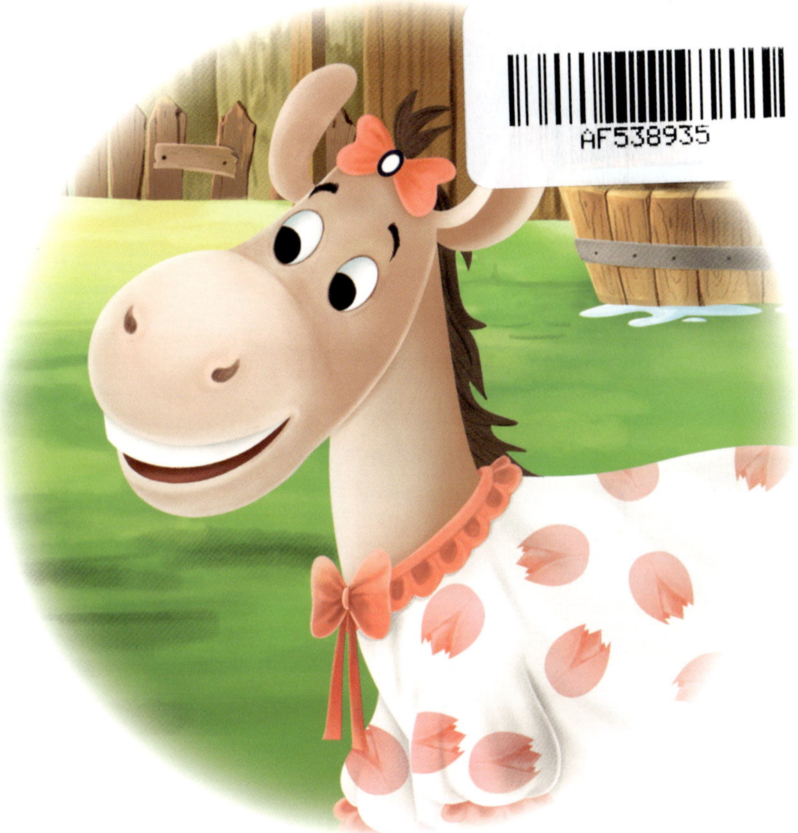

Om KIDZ
An imprint of Om Books International

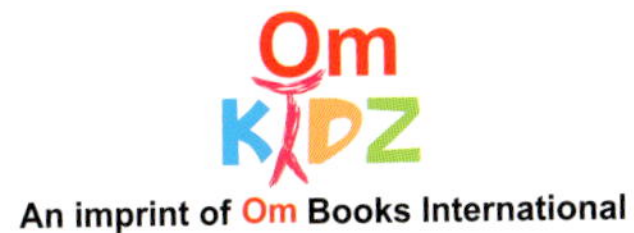

Reprinted in 2025

Corporate & Editorial Office
A-12, Sector 64, Noida 201 301
Uttar Pradesh, India
Phone: +91 120 477 4100
Email: editorial@ombooks.com
Website: www.ombooksinternational.com

Sales Office
107, Ansari Road, Darya Ganj
New Delhi 110 002, India
Phone: +91 11 4000 9000
Email: sales@ombooks.com
Website: www.ombooks.com

ISBN: 978-93-85273-82-7

Printed in India

10 9 8 7 6 5

The Cutest Mule

I'm all set to read

Paste your photograph here

My name is

There once was a farmer who **used** to work hard at his farm. He grew fruit from which his wife made lovely jam. The farmer had a **huge** barn where he stored all the fruit.

One day, the farmer went to his barn. He saw that one of his fruit baskets had toppled over. When he went to pick it up, it danced as if it could hear a **tune**!

The farmer was **confused**. "How can an empty basket dance?" he wondered. "It must be a clever ruse!"

The farmer decided to look closer. He was very **amused** when he picked up the basket. A baby **mule** was hiding under it! The baby **mule** looked **mutely** at the farmer.

The baby **mule** was very hungry. A **huge** tear rolled out of its eye. The farmer felt sorry for him and took him home.

The farmer's wife saw the baby **mule**. "Oh! Poor thing!" she exclaimed. "He needs a good scrubbing," she **mused**.

The baby **mule** looked **confused** as the farmer's wife prepared the bath. He **amused** himself with the bubbles. He loved the **perfume** of the soap. He played happily with the **tube** of toothpaste.

Once the bath was ready, the farmer's wife put the baby **mule** into the water. The little **mule** got scared. He hated the hot **fumes** that came out of the tub.

The farmer's wife was drenched as the baby **mule** splashed water all around. Chaos **ensued**, but the farmer got an idea and went to fetch his flute.

The farmer started playing the flute. The **music** calmed down the baby **mule**. The farmer's wife could finally give it a bath.

After the bath, the farmer's wife dried the baby **mule** with a towel. The baby **mule** watched her **mutely**. It felt good after a nice scrubbing.

The farmer's wife wanted to dress up the baby **mule**. The farmer **refused**, but the wife insisted. They had a **dispute**.

Finally, they decided to give it a try. The farmer's wife dressed up the baby **mule** in a white frock. It had **tulips** on it. The farmer looked on **amused**.

The farmer laughed at the pretty baby **mule**. "This is the **cutest mule** I have ever seen!" he said. The little **mule** looked pleased with his new **costume**.

Know your phonic words

These words have the long "u" sound in them.

used
tune
confused
amused
mule
mutely
huge
mused
perfume
tube
fumes
ensued
music
refused
dispute
tulips
cutest
costume